Of the People

Abraham Lincoln (1809–1865) was the 16th President of the United States (1860–1865). Lincoln successfully led America through its greatest crisis, the American Civil War. While preserving the Union, he abolished slavery and spurred modern industrialization of the country. His "Gettysburg Address" (1863) is considered the most eloquent speech in American history. It reflects America's dedication to the principles of equal rights, democracy, and liberty.

Tom Gerou

Late Intermediate

MOUNT RUSHMORE

Tom Gerou

Washington Fanfare

Of the People

The Rough Riders

The Architect

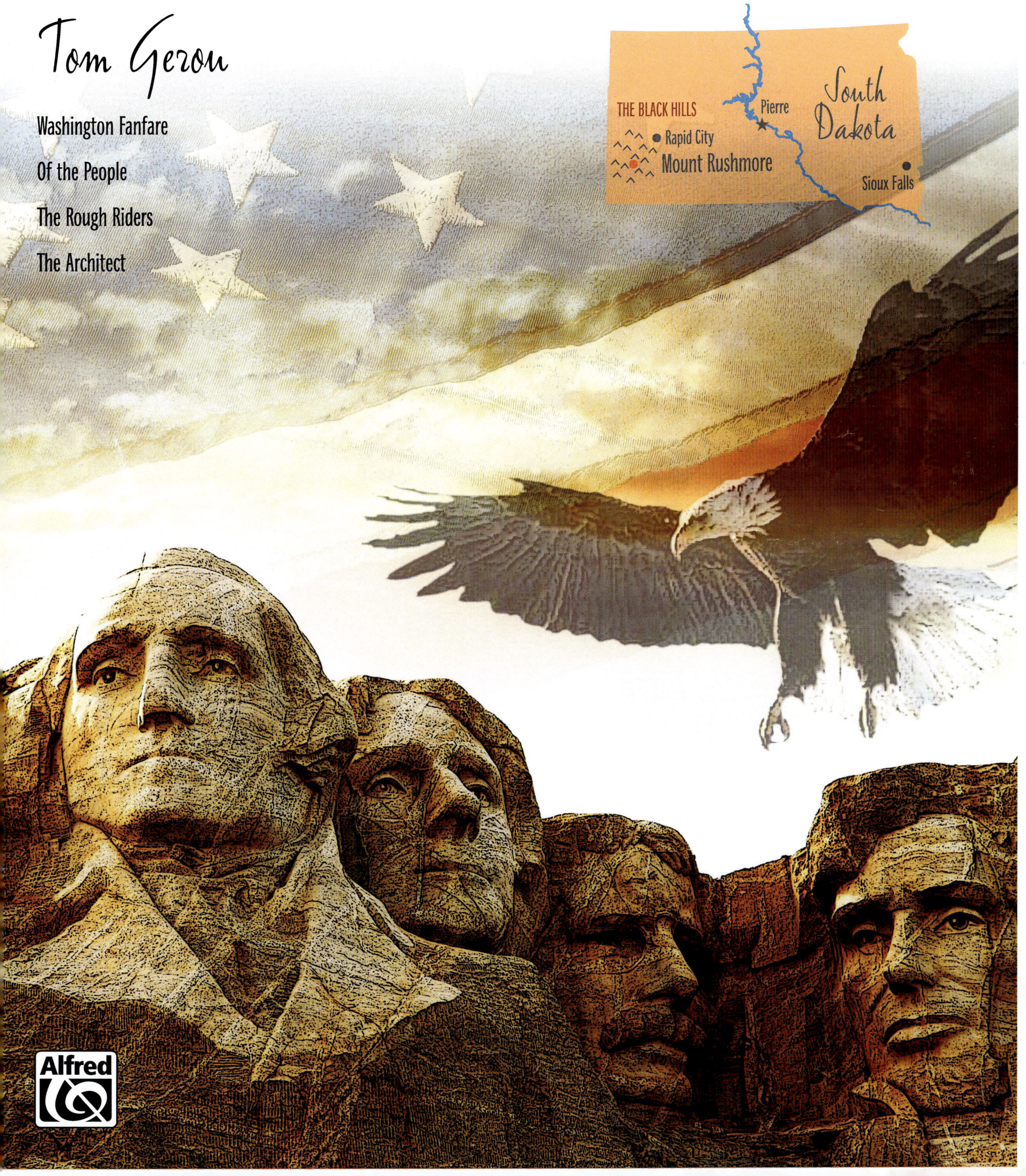

THE BLACK HILLS

Pierre

South Dakota

● Rapid City
Mount Rushmore

● Sioux Falls

Alfred

Washington Fanfare

George Washington (1732–1799), a Founding Father, was the first President of the United States (1789–1797), and the commander-in-chief of the Continental Army during the American Revolutionary War. He also presided over the convention that drafted the Constitution. Washington, along with Thomas Jefferson, Theodore Roosevelt, and Abraham Lincoln, is considered one of the top-ranking Presidents.

Tom Gerou

The Rough Rider

Theodore Roosevelt (1858–1919) was the 26th President of the United States of America (1901–1909). He was known for his exuberant personality and his mascaline "wild west" persona. Roosevelt was the youngest President ever, being 42 years old when sworn in as President. However, his achievements as an author, explorer, hunter, and naturalist are as much a part of his fame as any office he held as a politician. When the Spanish–American War broke out in 1898, he resigned from heading the Department of the Navy and formed a volunteer cavalry regiment called the Rough Riders that found fame fighting in Cuba.

Tom Gerou

Rugged and unbridled (♩. = 140)

The Architect

Thomas Jefferson (1743–1826) was the third President of the United States (1801–1809), one of the Founding Fathers, and the principal author of the Declaration of Independence (1776). He spoke five languages and developed deep interests in architecture, invention, religion, philosophy, and science. After being elected president, Jefferson oversaw the purchase of the vast Louisiana Territory from France (1803). He then sent the Lewis and Clark Expedition (1804–1806) to explore the new west.

Tom Gerou

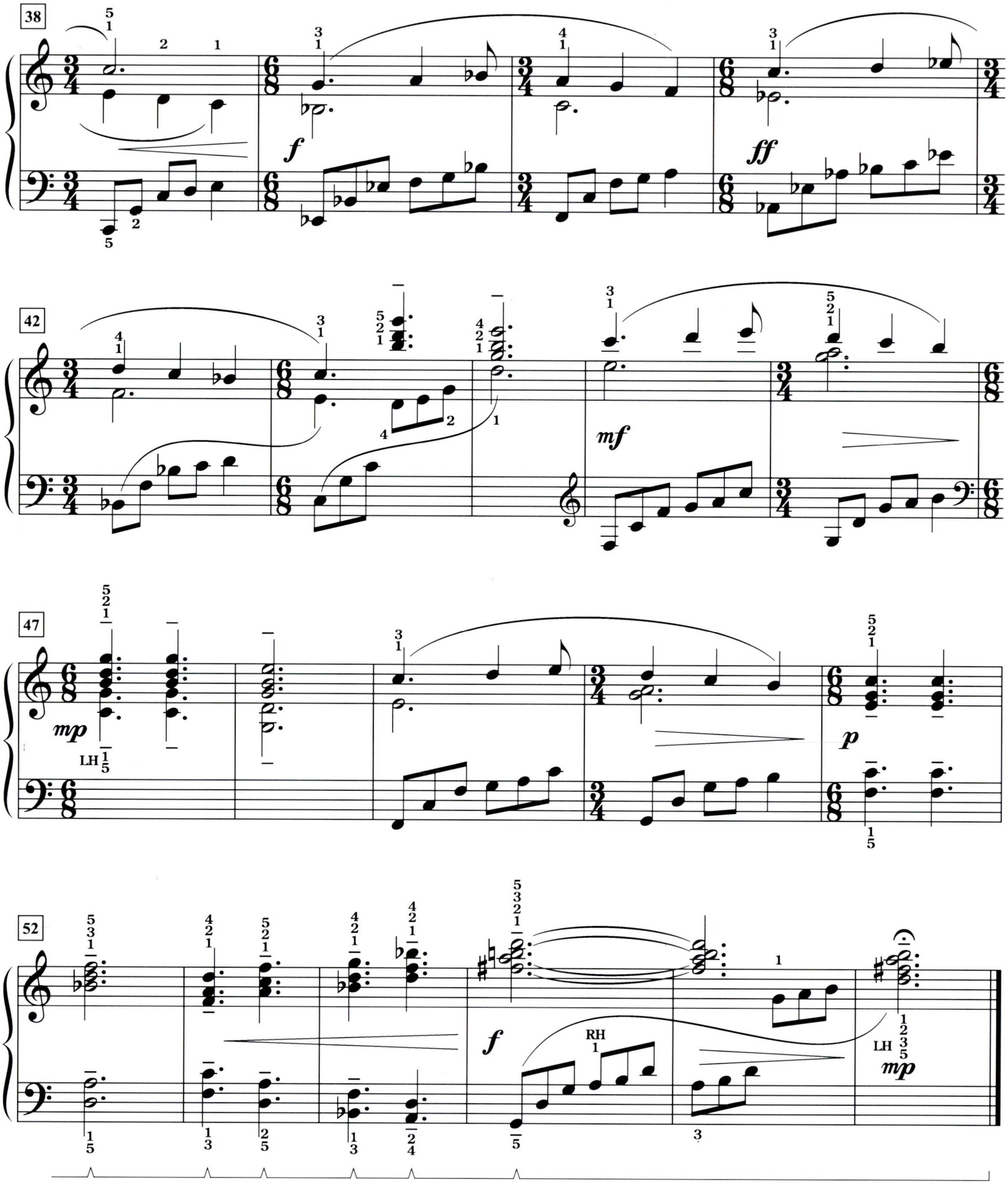

40627

ISBN-10: 0-7390-9428-9
ISBN-13: 978-0-7390-9428-0

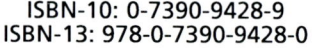

Alfred

alfred.com

40627 $5.50 in USA

ISBN 0-7390-9428-9